Fear of Knives
A BOOK OF FABLES

Anne Szumigalski

ILLUSTRATED *by* MARIE ELYSE ST. GEORGE

FOREWORD *by* JOHN LIVINGSTONE CLARK

HAGIOS
PRESS

The publishers gratefully acknowledge the support of
the Saskatchewan Arts Board in the publication of this
book.

Edited by John Livingstone Clark
Cover drawing by Marie Elyse St. George
Cover, design, and layout by Donald Ward
Set in Caslon by Ward Fitzgerald Editorial Design

Printed and bound in Canada

Canadian Cataloguing in Publication Data

Szumigalski, Anne, 1922-1999

   Fear of Knives

   ISBN 0-9682256-5-9

I. St. George, Elyse Yates, 1929-   II. Title.

PS8587.Z44 F3 2000   C813'.54   C00-920222-6
PR9199.3.S997 F3 2000

Fear of Knives

Contents

List of Drawings, Etchings, and Paintings

Cover: *Lions Know*, drawing, graphite on paper, 23.5 x 19.7 cm, 1999. Collection of the artist.

Page 8: *Otters*, drypoint etching, 51.0 x 35.6 cm, 1978. Collection of the artist.

Page 29: *Otters*, detail, drypoint etching, 28.0 x 15.25 cm, 1978. Collection of the artist.

Page 36: *Feral Child*, painting, acrylic on board, 10.0 x 7.5 cm, 1993. Private Collection.

Page 56: *Magic Cat*, drawing, graphite and charcoal on paper, 47.0 x 30.5 cm, 1990. Collection of the artist.

Page 60: *Gooseberry Fool*, detail, collaborative paper envelope painted with acrylic, containing recipes, herbal remedies, and autograph dialogue by Anne Szumigalski, approximately 30.5 x 45.75 cm, 1998. Private collection.

Page 80: *Himself and the Virgin*, drawing, graphite on paper, 10.0 x 7.5 cm, 1996. Collection of the artist.

Page 92: *Found Object*, moth specimen, approximately 16.5 x 12.0 cm, gift to M. E. St. George from Anne Szumigalski, 1996.

Page 97: *Deer Woman and Rat Queen*, painting, acrylic on board, 10.0 x 7.5 cm, 1992. Collection of Susan Whitney.

Page 104: *Otters*, detail, drypoint etching, 5.0 x 7.6 cm, 1978. Collection of the artist.

Foreword

And so we come to this little book, *Fear of Knives*, the last complete manuscript from the pen of Anne Szumigalski. There will be other publications, of course, bearing her name—I know that she had been working on a children's novel, and that it was almost finished at the time of her death. And there are plays extant in various stages, one of which was to be performed only in swimming pools. "Have you ever noticed," she once asked me, "how many of my titles have something to do with water? Now why do you think that is?" And surely there's bound to be more poetry. But *Fear of Knives* is the last manuscript that she edited and revised herself. Only the art has been added to what she provided us with in the early weeks of 1999. Anne's past collaboration with her long-time friend Marie Elyse St. George had produced such a lovely work—*Voice* —why not reunite them one last time? After all, greatness demands a special gesture, and there is no question in many of our minds that Anne Szumigalski was a great writer.

I was recently asked by a TV interviewer what made Anne so special, and my reply went something like this. She was so very exceptional on so many levels. Some poets, for example, are great with image and detail; some are musically inclined and have a strong sense of rhythm; some have formidable intellects and have penetrating ideas; and some have expansive and far-reaching imaginations. As a poet, you're lucky if you get a couple of these gifts. Szumigalski had them all: the imagery, the music, the intellect, and the imagination. She wove a rich tapestry of language that pulled colours and shapes from all over the cosmos and from every level of experience.

The same person then asked how I would sum up such a complex and talented person. My sense is that for her—and here I'm reaching back to the many conversations I enjoyed at her Saskatoon home—the four most operative words were Passion, Intelligence, Risk, and Imagination. She had no use for writing that was flaccid or anemic; life is meant to be lived full throttle, and that means passionately. Intelligence for Anne meant being sensitive to and curious about the world around us: nature, history, the mind and spirit. She was tremendously curious about everything, and had a far-ranging intellect that acquired languages, scientific information, philosophical ideas, and practical knowledge like a snowball rolling down a steep hill. Risk was essential for poetry because it was how you remained true to the promptings and stirrings of your inner being, your imagination: how you pushed the limits of convention and discovered new knowledge. For example, she once said that every time she started a new poem she felt like she was entering a new reality. Risk is also how the poet serves the tribe—the bard as prophet or shaman facing the awful (one of her favourite words) and mysterious abyss to bring back news for the community. And finally, Imagination: the faculty that she often thought was most neglected in Canadian writing, what with our "realist" fixation with hewers of words; in accordance with that, her favourite poet, as she reminded us constantly, was William Blake, or "Mr. B." For Blake and Szumigalski, Imagination was what brought you out of a fallen and illusory world of repressed and dehumanized feeling, thought, and perception.

Passion and Risk lead to confrontation, of course, and Anne—as a good dialectician—loved nothing more than a good fight, whether with other writers, academics, or politicians. If she thought the NDP (her party of choice) was cutting back on arts funding, there was Anne facing down Premier Roy Romanow at some public function. Even as she sat waiting for her final operation, she was firmly behind the striking nurses. She knew all too well from her wartime experiences the importance and difficulties of that profession. Anne gave herself tirelessly to people and to good causes; for example, she was there with a hilarious act for every 25th Street Theatre fund-raiser. Who will ever forget her as Edith Frumpole, Victorian baglady and poetess, sending up poets (and herself), politicians, and people in general? And never try to tell her that the arts are not an essential service. She'd send you running with salvos of hard logic charged with the most perfect elocution, vowels as round as cannonballs.

On the night before she died, I gave a reading at a local bookstore with three other poets. We each had differing definitions of poetry and, because my father had just passed away, I said that poetry is also commemorative. I then read poems for my father, and, because Anne was in hospital, a suite of poems I'd written for her. Early the next morning someone called to inform me that Anne was dead. None of us had a chance to say good-bye, and perhaps that's what hurts the most. She was uncomfortable with sentimentality and gushy emotion—typically English in that respect— but it would have been nice to tell her how much we loved her. In eternity I suspect she knows.

John Livingstone Clark
Dundurn, Saskatchewan
September 2000

Foreword

Artist's Statement

Anne and I often talked about drawing and painting. We'd discuss imagination, risk, form, discipline, and how to skirt the tar pits of self-indulgence and pretension. Simplicity and clarity, we felt, should be able to carry invention and imagination when artfully employed. She avoided the term "creative," and thought of writing as gardening. "You plant, prune, rearrange, and unearth what is latent there." Perhaps this is also true of visual art. You dig, rearrange shapes, colours, and elements until the image comes close to satisfying the need that engendered it.

Anne had a discerning eye for all art, and loved drawings in particular. She was interested in why and how I approached a work. During our several collaborations, she was often the first to see a new piece of mine, and I'd watch her face for that *frisson* of excitement I hoped would be there.

I greatly miss our mutual enthusiasms, explorations, laughs, and arguments.

My work is usually a reaction to a text or events that interest me. The cover drawing, *Lions Know*, from Anne's fable "Gerald," is one she would have enjoyed. The lioness wonders, what's all this mystery about words? Life is simply birth, hunger, mating, and death.

Himself and The Virgin, a study for a painting of an adolescent on the ambivalent cusp of womanhood, was named after reading Anne's poem.

She wrote "Ferret" after seeing *Feral Child*, which I painted in response to an article about an urban feral child in the *New Yorker*.

The other works are serendipitous finds.

Marie Elyse St. George
Saskatoon, Saskatchewan
September 2000

Artist's Statement

A Man Looks Down

into the handsome blue eyes of the woman he is making love to. In her left eye he is surprised to see a tiny man very like himself. Only this one is fully dressed in corduroy trousers and a blue jacket and is sitting dejectedly on a three-legged stool. His arms are folded across his chest.

The woman blinks her eyes, and it seems to the man that her dark lashes are the bars of a jail cell that the tiny fellow is locked up in. You have a prisoner in your left eye, says the man to his mistress. She doesn't understand, but imagines that the remark must be some sort of compliment, for after all he *is* making love to her, and so she smiles vaguely and ecstatically up at him. How happy I am with you, she murmurs.

The man cannot take his mind off the unfortunate little captive, but still he *is* in the act of making love. And so he moans softly to show the woman how much pleasure she is giving him.

When the woman again opens her eyes she sees her lover leaning over her gazing intently at her face. Come here, he says brusquely; he takes her head roughly between his hands and jerks it toward him. The woman is startled at his coldness and violence. She begins to weep with indignation. Keep still, you bitch, shouts the man.

When at last he manages to hold down her head and turn back her left eyelid there is nothing there but a blue eye its edges red with fury. The man has never felt so chagrined. He scrabbles about amongst the bed-clothes searching desperately for the tears his mistress has just shed, for perhaps the little man, who looked so much like himself, is drowning somewhere between the crumpled sheets.

Anne Szumigalski

A Herring Lives in the Sea

He's pretty sure it's the sea, though after all there are such creatures as freshwater herrings. All he can see is the clear green water above, and beneath him the murky sand, and of course the tails of the fishes that swim before him in his particular school.

It is his joy and despair to live out his life among so many of his fellows, for what could be more exciting than the swoosh of synchronized movement as the whole group dashes in and out of drowned wrecks and kelp forests like a silvery sinuous breeze?

Not that everything is certain for a herring. This one swims always in the centre of the school and therefore cannot be sure whether he is following those in front or being chased by those behind. Both, perhaps.

A fish swimming in a school has the fortune, or the misfortune, to be at the same time a completely social animal and a completely solitary one. This at least gives him the opportunity for conjecture and speculation, while at the same time he is exercising his shining body and delicate fins. It is like being a hermit, he decides, and at the same time a not-unimportant member of a tight community. The fish consoles himself with the knowledge that some monasteries, both Christian and Bhuddist, work on the same principle.

Nevertheless, any creature may sometimes stray, and one day, for one reason or another, the herring lags behind his fellows and drops out of the stream of things for just a moment.

The school happens to be passing over a reef at the time, and a large grouper darts out of its lair and snaps him up in one gulp.

And so the herring has left one entity to become part of another, part of a large and very solitary fish with a huge mouth and a wide lazy body. The grouper lurks all day and night under its stony shelf, waiting for unwary creatures to stray from their appointed places. Snap go its toothy jaws as it swallows this one and that into its roomy stomach. The herring—who is now assimilated into the grouper—can't help being somewhat amused at his fate. Now he has become a solitary creature who is yet an integral part of the reef on which he lives, and on which he depends. Does nothing ever really change for any of God's creatures? It is a wonder, he thinks, that the Almighty hasn't bored Himself out of existence long ago.

Anne Szumigalski

A Man Is Standing

at the deal table in the kitchen of his house in Regina. He has his back to the door. He is cutting the flesh from the carcass of a gazelle. The only knife heavy enough to do the job is a serrated bread knife. All the others are too small or too blunt.

He has dragged this dead animal all the way from Africa, where his dream took him while he was napping on the couch in the living room. After the trouble and danger and desire of the hunt, he was loathe to leave the lovely thing to be devoured by crows and blowflies, or other scavengers—hyenas perhaps? He does, indeed, remember strange cries in the distance on the veldt. His reluctance, of course, is partly due to the fact that he does not want to admit to all the scavenging that his humdrum life has forced upon him, for during his afternoon of sleep and reflection the pure idea of the hunt has become so dear to him that he simply cannot bring himself to relinquish his prey.

The skin of the animal, which he has flayed with unexpected skill, now lies on the worn linoleum under the old-fashioned table his wife is so fond of. She brought it from her grandmother's abandoned farm-house when the old lady died last year. Just the very perfect thing, she had said. Of course she had brought other things from there: two plants with leaves greying at the edges which she hoped to save from root rot or whatever it was that was bothering them, and a shot glass decorated with small enamel pigs which got larger as the glass got taller. The more booze you give your-self, she explained, the bigger pig you are. Her husband with a smile had said he could have guessed that, but what if you were pouring it for someone else? Surely that would inhibit your guest, whoever he was. *She*, said his wife with a little grunt, which could have been either yes or no, or perhaps that she was imitating the smallest of the enamel pigs. The man had wisely found it best not to pursue this thought.

Now the table is stained with pinkish blood, not at all like human blood, he tells himself. But what does he know about that? He who has always been so careful with sharp instruments and has never once cut himself, or anyone else for that matter. Now he looks down at his hands sticky with the life-blood of this animal that had sprung so gracefully before him across the land-scape of his dream. It was partly this grace that had spurred him to the hunt. He had surprised himself by suddenly becoming fleet of foot. In fact, he remem-bered watching his swiftly running feet as they carried him with certainty across the short grass and through the low bushes. On and on until he could hardly breathe for joy as he levelled what must have been some sort of spear to bring the animal down.

Where is that spear now? He can't remember having

　　　　　　　　　　　Anne Szumigalski

pulled it out of the animal's wounded neck. But he must have because when he had triumphantly dragged the carcass across the threshold of his dream, his weapon was nowhere to be seen, just the gaping wound in the creature's neck. That cry he had heard: was it the voice of the dying animal or the shout of success from his own throat?

Now he begins to worry about cleaning up the kitchen when all this butchering is done, for, in spite of her predilection for the old and worn—or perhaps because of it—his wife is an enthusiastic housekeeper, given to a great deal of mopping and scrubbing. What will she say about this mess?

Just as he thinks of her, his wife comes in and throws down the car keys on the table, on the only bit of table that is not covered with guts and butchered flesh. Your turn for the chariot, she says cheerfully. Marion is picking me up for the meeting. Don't forget it's your choir night, and she turns neatly on the heels of her good shoes and leaves.

What should he do now? Should he phone the Reverend and explain that he's busy cutting up a slain African antelope? There are only two other tenors. That'll leave the sound a bit thin, but he is engrossed with the small deer-like creature before him on the table. O tiny hooves and fine thready sinews. Can anything in Earth or Heaven be as delicate as its teeth, as soft as its turned-out lip? Well, he must forget about everything but the task he has set himself.

It takes a full hour, but it's done at last. The meat is all packaged and the lovely head buried in the compost pile. But what to do with the skin? He takes one of the small blunt knives and scrapes away at it, then wets it and stretches it and fastens it with four nails to the garden door.

In the end he can't help glorying in his skill. He fills a bucket, takes a brush and a bar of soap and begins the task of cleaning the table and the floor. And while he works he sings:

> vos flores rosarum qui in effusione sanguinis vesti beati estis.*

He remembers the words so clearly. The music is more difficult, though. He has to run through it several times before he gets it exactly right.

* You blossoming roses
 how blessed you are in the outpouring of your blood.
 Hildegard von Bingen
 "Hymn to the Martyrs"

Anne Szumigalski

A Catechism (or Conversation)

PHON *and* ANTIPHON

Ph.   It's true, isn't it, that to return to God is to come
back to oneself?

Ant.   Self, self, what self is that?

Ph.   The endowment, the name, speech and seeds.
You could call it voice.

Ant.   Who gave you this voice?

Ph.   I was given it in the beginning. I was born blind as
a kitten and could not see the face of the great
Donor.

Ant.   Were you deaf, too? Tell me about His voice.

Ph.   I can tell you this much—there was no indication
that the Donor is male.

Ant.   Female then?

Ph.   Not particularly.

Ant.   A child then?

Ph.   Not particularly.

Ant.   A Crocodile?

Ph.   Possibly.

Ant.   So what did the Great Crocodile say? I suppose
you can at least remember that?

Ph.   Difficult. The Voice was kind of growly.

Ant.   Aha, I thought so, a male crocodile.

Ph.   You think female crocodiles have soprano voices? Are there operas, then, on the banks of the Nile?

Ant.   *Aida.*

Ph.   So God spoke—sang—to me in Italian you think?

Ant.   Perhaps that's the reason . . .

Ph.   . . . for what?

Ant.   For how hard to understand those words were.

Ph.   I tried my very best, but . . . how about you? Did you understand those first words?

Ant.   How could I, I who was born deaf as a bat?

Ph.   Bats aren't deaf.

Ant.   How do you know?

Ph.   I read it in a book.

Ant.   What book? Anyway, you said you were born blind.

Ph.   I got my sight when my mother took me to the Holy Spring.

Ant.   Did she dip you in?

Ph.   I'll say. The water was fucking cold.

Ant.   (*piously*) We're in the sight, hearing of the Sacred Reptile, who may not want to be subjected to your vulgarities.

Ph.   In the sight of God all words are holy. It says so in the Bible.

Ant.   The f-word isn't in the Bible.

Ph.   It's in the Anglo Saxon Bible.

Ant.   So now God is an Anglo Saxon crocodile?

Ph.   There's no evidence to the contrary.

Ant.   There are no crocodiles in the Thames.

Ph.   Not now, but there used to be. Teeth have been found, and the remnants of a scaly tail.

Ant.   A likely tale.

                                         Anne Szumigalski

Ph. As likely as any other. As likely as our existence.
Ant. Or our persistence, these centuries.
Ph. These many years.
Ant. These days.
Ph. These long moments.
Ant. Glitches.
Ph. Hitches.
Ant. To the trousers of time.

On Yarn

She's learning to knit, and the young man behind the counter at Kathy's Krafts is persuading her of the satisfaction to be gained from working in wool. You can make such lovely lumpy things with it, he explains, to hang on the wall or give the cat to play with. Lately, though, there has been a return to the cult of usefulness. That means you must be able to use and/or wear everything you knit up.

Or crochet, she says in her heart. No wonder so many people go around in coats that should be blankets and hats like tea cosies. As for those pepper-and-salt skirts with bits of stick woven into them, who knows, they may be hammocks in their spare time.

The man leans his elbows on the counter and leans intimately toward her. To tell the truth, he says in a low voice, I find that working it up takes away the threat of infinity that lurks in every skein and ball. If you stop to think of those miles and miles of worsted going on and on without a break, or even a thin weak spot, it gives you the dizzies. But when at last your needles and hooks have eaten it all up, no matter how long the labour or enormous the garment, there is the end, tiny and limp.

Anne Szumigalski

The Margin

One morning in late spring a young woman wakens alone on a strange shore. When she sits up and looks about her, she sees that she has been sleeping in the sheltered hollow between two sand hills. All around her the low dunes are spread with patches of sea-holly and spike grass. Because it's not yet summer, the grass is still sharply green and the holly's glaucus leaves are still pliant in their papery bracts.

She gets to her feet and looks eastward. At first all she can see is endless quilted sand, but when she shades her eyes and looks into the sun she can just make out a narrow strip of ocean glittering in the brilliant light. It is as though the sea were a snail which has felt the land's thrust as the prod of a finger and has shrunk back immediately into its shell of pearly sky and distance.

The woman has no idea where she has come from. All she knows is that the journey took many days, weeks perhaps, even a month. She has travelled from a great city in another country, but has forgotten the name of that place, the names of her companions, even her own name. She is ragged and travel-weary, but happier than she has ever dreamed of being.

> My hands are fishes
> Loosed from the angler's barb

she sings clearly in a language she has never heard before,

> My feet are otters
> Sprung from the trap.

Some time later, she tells herself, she may bring to mind that other place, those other people, that other language. But for now she is content to wander on the beach, foraging for food, and naming everything she sees in the new words which come so freely to her tongue.

Anne Szumigalski

The Funnel

There once was a young girl who was very good with her needle. That is to say, she could make almost anything that her mother suggested—providing she had the proper materials, of course.

And they prospered, the mother and the daughter, the mother buying the yard goods and the needles and the threads and taking in the orders, the daughter, she of the sharp eyes and the delicate fingertips, working on the fine stitching and pleating that the customers demanded.

One day, as the girl sat sewing in the garden as usual, a strange feeling came over her. No wonder she felt a little faint and dizzy: for the first time in her life an idea of her own had come to her mind. At last, at last a project of her own, and however long it took she was determined to bring it to be. She, who had always been in the habit of calling her mother every half hour or so to come and give her opinion on the delicacy of her embroidery or the almost invisible stitching of her hems, now fell silent. All afternoon she sat in the shade of the laburnum tree, bent over her work, without a single word passing her lips.

Anne Szumigalski

Several times her mother came to the garden door to make sure that the girl was not dozing in the warmth of the afternoon sun, but when she saw her so closely and happily employed with her sewing she concluded that all was well and she took up her basket and went down to the village shop to buy a few little things and to pick up any sewing orders that had come in during the past day or two.

As for the daughter, she was happy to be working at last on something that had nothing whatever to do with her mother or her aunts or any of the other stuffy old ladies of the town. Once she had thought the thing out to her satisfaction and rummaged in her scrap bag for the necessary materials, her fingers flew about her work, and she was surprised when at last she looked up that the afternoon had gone by and dusk was already falling.

Of course it took her more than one day to perfect this thing, this wonderful construct of linen and wire and lace and embroidery thread that she had decided to call the Funnel of Time. It meant a good deal of care and thought on her part, for the thing had to be small enough to fit in her apron pocket yet large enough for her purpose. In the end, she managed to make it of such supple and translucent material that she could carry it with her always and not be too obvious about it.

The way it worked was this: if she held the small end to her left eye and stared through it, she could go back in time and revisit the scenes of her childhood. This was endlessly amusing to her, as, like most of us, she couldn't remember much before she was about five, and so a great many of her happiest days were lost to her. Now she could relive them all: the day she first sat up and viewed the world from something higher than a pillow, the day of her first tentative steps, and so on and so on; the time when her father gave her her first doll, he picked her up in his arms and hugged her and put the doll, a rag baby with yellow tow hair, into her hands.

The doll's name, she now remembered, was Angelina. It had been a difficult name for a little child to master, but she had tried her best. In the end, she had called the doll Banjy, and she had carried it with her everywhere for a couple of years until its yellow hair had almost all fallen out, and several small holes had appeared on its rag face. What a terrible day that had been when Banjy had to be discarded. She had cried and cried, and when her Uncle Joe had tried to comfort her with a quite beautiful toy giraffe, she had thrown the silly thing across the room and flung herself down on the floor and drummed with her heels until she began to enjoy the drumming and had quite forgotten why she was doing it.

And so the memories of childhood were not all happy ones, and the young woman decided to find out what would happen if she looked through the wide end of the funnel. She clapped this to her right eye and the result was equally interesting; now she could go forward in time. A far more dangerous journey, as anyone could have told her.

At first her interest was caught by the joy of her wedding eve, and then of the wedding itself. Would it really be like this, she wondered. It was only when she found herself pregnant with her first child that she realized that yes, there was a reality about all this. By now she was not just a spectator, but was actually living

Anne Szumigalski

through the experiences of her future. This was too much. Things were rushing forward far too quickly. She wanted to stop and savour some of the happier days, playing with her little children, getting her teenage daughter ready for her first dance—that kind of thing. But time just dashed on. What was she to do? How could she put an end to all this? She struggled with the funnel, which seemed to be stuck to her eye and impossible to dislodge, but at last, after a great effort, she was able to pull the thing away and fling it into a rosebush.

The woman gave a great sigh of relief. At least she had not had to go on to the very end of her life, and perhaps even beyond, but now that she had thrown away the contraption, she knew that she could not go back in time. She was stuck where she was, still in her garden, which was blossoming as always. She thought she recognized the two little girls who were playing bat and ball on the grass. But when one of them called out, Gran, Gran come and play with us, she realized that these were not her children at all, but her grandchildren. Her hands when she looked at them were rather worn and wrinkled, and when she ran to join the children she was a bit slower than she expected to be. She had to admit the truth. She was stuck with being an old woman.

There was nothing she could do about it. It was a fact. She would have to accept the inevitable and live out the rest of her life as best she could.

And so she set about being the best grandmother she knew how and dearly did she love the little girls who were her joy and delight.

One day, when the eldest girl was about ten years old, she was helping her grandmother weed the garden when she spied something caught among the thorns of the rosebush. Yes, it was the Funnel of Time which had been thrown there those many years ago.

When the grandmother saw what the child had found, a cold fear gripped her whole being and she tried to wrench the offending object from the child's hand. The girl, however, would not let it go. What was the poor woman to do? Nothing for it but to explain what this thing was and to warn her granddaughter of its terrible powers.

She held out her hand to take the Funnel, but the girl still wouldn't give it up. She just laughed in the old woman's face. Don't be silly, Gran, said the young one, still laughing, Time is just a game, and this thing is just a toy, and she threw it up into the clear ultimate sky.

The grandmother and the granddaughter watched the Funnel until it disappeared into the blue, but though they stared up, straining their eyes for several minutes, they neither of them saw it fall, and though they searched and searched they never did find out in which part of the garden it had finally come to earth.

Anne Szumigalski

A Game

Across town a head appears sideways in a window. It is a polished head, bald as an acorn: its sagacious profile something we have always longed for.

At home we are playing a board game, "Man and Metaphor." The destiny of each little figure is held between a clumsy thumb and a numb finger. Delicate are the ways of such small creatures, I remark.

As you slide Bluewoman, and I slide Redman, up and down the golden ladders, they collide and retreat, turn and return. And yet, you say, we are wholly at their mercy. The quirk of a smile turns up one corner of your mouth. Love is as biased as fear, I rejoin.

The head in the faraway window turns slowly to face us, winking its blank left eye, weeping with the other.

Ferret

The woman who lived on the edge of the moor looked up one morning from her sewing and her cup of clover tea. Had she imagined that sound, something between a child singing and the yip of a fox? Had she imagined that skipping shadow crossing the pathway that led into the woods beyond the garden?

It was not like the shadow of a wolf or a bear or any of the other wild creatures she saw quite often moving among the trees. Sometimes these were friendly and sometimes they were menacing. She knew them all by sight and did not disturb their lives, nor they hers.

But this presence was of a different kind, and she waited to see what or who approached her house. But the shadow flitted away and was gone among the trees.

Next day, and the day after that, the woman saw the shadow again, but still she had not seen the creature who owned it. On the third day, however, when she looked up from her work, she saw a young boy standing on the pathway. He was thin as a deer, and his hair hung raggedly down about his shoulders like the mane of a wolf. He was naked as a nestling, and his eyes were like the eyes of a hawk seeking its prey.

The woman called out to the child who, at the sound of her human voice, immediately vanished into the woods. But still after that he came every day to her dooryard, and she fed him birdseed and chopped roots and gave him goat's milk to drink.

Time passed and the boy became a little more friendly. On nights of sharp frost he even came into the house to sleep. Not that he would lie in a bed. He slept on a pile of straw in the corner furthest from the stove, for it was obvious he was mortally afraid of the fire.

As the weeks and the months went by, the woman and the boy became accustomed to one another. She cut his hair neatly around his head, and every morning she called him to sit at her feet while she combed out the knots and the tangles and the burrs and the twigs. She took his measure and made him a rough country smock and breeches. She even taught him to say a few words in his strange voice which was like the cry of a raucous bird, but he was never able to tell her who he was or how he came to live wild in the forest.

As for his eyes, they were piercing as a pigeon-hawk's, and indeed some afternoons he went into the woods and caught rabbits or small birds for the pot. When the woman found these offerings laid at her feet as though by a faithful hound, she skinned and plucked them and even managed to teach her wild boy which herbs to bring from the garden to add to the stew. She would sit down at the table to eat with a napkin across her knee, but he took his portion into the yard and devoured it straight from the gravelly dirt without benefit of even so much as a tin plate. As she daintily cut the meat from the bones, she tried to forget the toothmarks at the throat of the prey. And so she named

Anne Szumigalski

the boy Ferret, and that was the name he would answer to when she called him to her.

A year passed and the wild boy and the quiet woman got used to one another. In fact, she had almost begun to think of him as her son. But that was not to last. One spring day he simply disappeared into the woods and did not return. When dusk fell she walked a little way among the trees calling his name. There was no sign of him that night, or the next, and when she found the clothes she had made for him dropped in a heap on the back doorstep, she knew in her heart that her feral boy had gone back to the wild and would never return to her.

Once more she was left to her solitary pursuits of sewing and sweeping and baking and brewing tea. Mornings, as she sat in her window, she would glance up every so often at the garden and the forest beyond, hoping, yet not daring to hope, for one more glimpse of that shadow on the dirt path, longing to hear once more that strange cry, something between a howl and a song.

A Girl Dreams

of a sleeping man. She leans forward as though over the open roof of her dollhouse and watches the man's dream.

The girl is lying in her bed in the nursery on the top floor of a house more than two hundred years old. Within her lies the man she has dreamed up. He is careful not to disturb her. He breathes to the very same rhythm she does, turns when she turns, tries to synchronize his heartbeat with hers. Their double breath is exhaled through the child's nostrils, and ascends to the ceiling, where a ring of painted plaster cherubs prances around a frosted glass lamp. The breath of generations of children has smeared the cherubs' colours; they have become grey and chalky.

The girl is fast asleep, but she has the sensation of opening her eyes and noticing the five little fellows with their ribbons and their garlands, then her sight turns inward once more, and she concentrates on the man, who is dreaming of a dog with a human head. Presently that changes, and he becomes a human boy with the head of a dog.

The dogboy is foolish enough to be happy about his new form; indeed, he is quite smug about it. This annoys the girl, and she wants to interfere at once and change the dogperson into someone more curious, afraid and disenchanted.

She asks herself: does this creature yap, or does he speak? In his mind, does he lie pampered and useless in

Anne Szumigalski

a padded dog basket, or does he think of himself as a dangerous huskie sleeping out in the winter night under a quilt of snow?

She makes up her mind that he's far too tame for that, much tamer, in fact, than any ordinary boy. He shall lie in a wooden bed with muslin sheets, much like the one in her dollhouse, though bigger of course.

But is it right for her to make these decisions for him? After all, he is not in her dream; he belongs to the man. It is true that she has dreamed the man, but how far can she go? Does a man in a dream have free will? Does he have independent dreams, or do they in some way belong to her?

The girl thinks about this for some time. Your imagination is your own, she tells the man at last, but don't forget that you are bound to let me know all your dreams and conjectures. The rule is that I can see everything but I am not allowed to change it. This seems fair, and the man agrees.

Later, they begin to quarrel about whether the people in the man's dream are to be told that the girl is watching them and no doubt making her own judgements of their shapes and their deeds. It will make them happy, the girl argues, to know that I am interested in them, that from a distance I wish them well.

No, says the man firmly, they are never to hear of your existence, for they would be unable to accept your curiosity. Any more than you, dearest child, can accept the fact that one of those grubby little angels up there— I shall not tell you which—is watching and judging you, that with his faded blue eye he is following your every move.

The Sleigh

A boy one day decides to deceive his mother into letting him stay home from school. Most of us have tried this at one time or other, with varying degrees of success, but Sandor, the boy in question, has not so far made the attempt. This is mostly because he enjoys being at school, running around with a rough gang of boys a bit older than himself, terrorizing smaller children and playing tricks on the teachers.

It was this last activity which has prompted him to complain to his mother of a headache. Mr. Ballon, when he found the dead cat in his desk, had sworn to punish the culprits. As he said this he looked directly at Sandor. Does he really know who had done the terrible deed? Better, the boy thinks, to put at least one day between his teacher and the crime. By that time the other partners in sin can have been found out and punished, and perhaps the whole thing will have blown over.

His mother puts her hand sympathetically on the boy's forehead. No fever, she murmurs, more to herself than to her son. But perhaps he does look a little pale, certainly a little sorry for himself. Yes, she decides he shall stay home at least for this one day and see how things go.

Anne Szumigalski

But she is not quite as completely deceived as the boy would have liked. Probably an upset stomach, she says crisply. And she takes up her market basket and leaves, without giving the boy so much as a piece of dry toast for his breakfast. She's decided that he's not too sick to look after himself. After all, he's ten years old, and surely that's big enough to do without his mother's care for a few hours. As a matter of fact, she has made up her mind to look in at the school and find out from his teacher just what kind of trouble this son of hers has got himself into.

Her seeming indifference has only spurred Sandor on to greater feats of deception. As she leaves, she looks back at him as he sits on his bed by the window holding his head and making little moaning noises. She doesn't exactly slam the door behind her, but she does shut it a little more enthusiastically than usual.

As soon as he is sure that his mother is not likely to return and check on him, the boy jumps out of bed in search of something to eat. He rummages around in the kitchen and manages to find a loaf of bread and a jar of jam—his favourite, raspberry. These he takes back to his bed and begins to devour with gusto, his enforced fast having made him even more hungry than usual. When he finishes, he realizes he has eaten the whole thing, even scraping out the jam jar with a teaspoon. There is no way his mother won't notice what he's done, especially as the quilt is smeared and sticky with the jam, and, when he gets out of bed and brushes off the sheets, a scatter of pinkish breadcrumbs decorates the linoleum floor.

By this time his attention has been drawn to the view from the window. Why has he never noticed it before, he wonders. There is the garden with its rosebushes and petunia bed, and beyond that the park with its trees and its three swings. Come to that, he has spent a great deal of time in that park. Pushing the little ones off the swings and yelling obscenities at the familiar grandfather who is always to be found at dusk sitting on the green-painted bench by the fence, smoking his evening pipe. Not that he is any rougher or ruder than any of his friends. He is merely a boy with a boy's preoccupations.

It's the end of September already, and it is not too much of a surprise when it clouds over and begins to snow. Not much at first, but the flakes thicken quickly, and quite soon the park is almost hidden behind a curtain of whirling flakes. Sandor gives up the idea of taking a stroll and sits by the window. He presses his face against the glass, trying to see what can be going on there. By the time the blizzard stops, the ground is white with snow. Sandor's spirits, like those of any other boy, rise with the promise of the first snow of the year. He begins to wonder where his winter boots are, and his parka and his gloves. Perhaps if he rummages in the basement and in the attic he'll be able at least to run out and roll a few snowballs to throw at somebody— even if it's only the next-door cat.

Just then the snow abates to just a few floating flakes, and he sees something in the park he has never noticed before. An old horse, a small old horse almost no more than a pony, is dragging a sleigh across the snowy vista of the park. There are bells on the sleigh and Sandor is convinced he can hear them ringing as the horse trots along. But how can he? The

Anne Szumigalski

window is shut tight and there is the length of the garden between him and the park.

He opens the window to listen and the cold air blows against his face. The last of the snowflakes settle on his nose and eyelids. He has a fellow feeling with the horse, whose muzzle is frosted with white.

It's then that he notices the boy in the sleigh. When the child turns to face him, he sees that this boy is, in fact, himself. The same little ferrety face, the same buck teeth, the same freckles and gingery red hair.

If this is so, then the boy in the sleigh must be as astonished as he is to see his face at the window of the small house by the park. He must be.

Now Sandor realizes that this whole thing, his trick on his teacher, his mother's absence, his own pallor— all these have been arranged simply so that he might come face to face with himself and make his choice. Either he can decide to be the boy at the window looking out or the boy in the sleigh wrapped in the blanket looking in. He has just the few minutes to make up his mind. When the sleigh has passed, it is passed, that's all. It doesn't occur to him that if he decides to become the boy in the sleigh and be whisked off to places and lives unknown, then the boy in the sleigh will be bound to become the boy in the window, waiting with trepidation for his mother's return, for her turned-away face, for her cold voice as she berates him for his boyish pranks, but most of all for his attempt to deceive his dear mother, she who has given up her whole life for him, she who loves him as no one else will ever love him, wicked and ungrateful though he is.

Gerald

The spiritual advisor, he told us to call him Gerald, commanded us all to kneel. Most did so, but a few of us held out against a demand we felt to be humiliating. Then we were to put our hands on our heads as a token of submission. None of us did that. After all, why should we debase ourselves simply to please a power-hungry old man?

We were surprised when we heard his ancient cackle of a laugh, astonished when he praised the rebellious ones. Obedience can be a sin, he explained, in certain circumstances. We imagined a circle within which the more timid of us were trapped, but others ran boldly about and were not confined by any particular system of thought.

It took us only a day to realize that, in fact, we had all been bamboozled, for if we were disobedient again it could be concluded that we were confined by our need for praise, our slavish desire to please the hierophant. That's how we regarded him now, simply as an old teacher of orthodoxies, with all sorts of tricks up his sleeve to catch out any of us who leaned dangerously toward independent ideas.

Anne Szumigalski

Nothing, we knew, had changed since our world began, this small world of our studies, our constant striving toward the light. The path is dusty and the road is thorny. We knew that, of course, and we accepted as inevitable the sharp stones of Gerald's disapproval as we became a group united against the holy old reprobate.

He would try to conquer us; we would resist him. We held secret meetings to discuss all sorts of ways of cheating him.

Maddeningly, he appeared to take no notice. All these little venial sins are of no importance, he seemed to be telling us. Indeed, he forgave us everything. He beamed indulgently upon us. Can you imagine how infuriating this was? After all, we had not come here to be pandered to like a bunch of silly children.

It was then that we decided to separate. Perhaps we had misunderstood the dictum *divide and conquer*. Each of us took a different road to the destruction of the old man's argument. We forgot the words *united front, common purpose*, all that sort of rubbish. We were no longer a pack of wild dogs nipping at his ideas. Each of us became his own creature. We even went so far as to wear badges to denote our differences: a tiger, an anaconda, a rogue elephant. This last was, of course, myself. I felt huge wearing that badge. But I knew, as did the others, that we were now not just contending against our sainted master but against one another. We were each as likely to injure another student as we were to hurt His Reverence. Could a tiger, I constantly asked myself, leap upon the back of an elephant and sever its spine with one bite? If I, the elephant, were to step upon the scorpion, would her sting prove mortal to me, as my tread would certainly be to the venomous little arachnid?

Thus had the sly old master divided his enemies. Now he could conquer us one by one. We would not even want to call upon each other for help. Nothing could save us from the cage, the circle, the swap, and the sell-out.

And so he has won our souls, and we are obedient to him, though not slavishly so. For Gerald has left this world and left it to us, his students. As we watch an old woman grinding his bones on the mountainside, we are brought to the realization that his dust and the taste of it pervades all of us. We eat him. We breathe him. We take up into our own bones the Geraldessence which will certainly divide us and pollute us, as much as it will bring us together and make us one.

Anne Szumigalski

The Almshouse

In our village time has come to an end. There is no more of it. All around us they have built a wall of translucent glass brick. When you strain your eyes you can just see the shadows of farmers mounted on tractors tilling the fields out there. As they move back and forth they flicker against the eye.

As time has come to an end, there is neither night nor day. Light and darkness are intermittent.

The children, of course, are not called to bed, and the shouts of their play hang in the air like so many moons of dust. I sit on a bench near the playground. I glance at my feet side by side on the grass. My shoes are dull and cracked; the frayed laces have been mended again and again. They are old, but no older than they will ever be.

The Flight

At the beginning of winter an old woman lies dying in her cottage at the end of a village. In her extremity she is enlightened and can clearly see not only all the details of the life she is now leaving, but every moment of every day of all the lives she has led since God created her.

The thing that impresses her most is the deathbed of the life immediately before this one. That time she was a man, one who had made a great name for himself in this world.

The famous man lies in a large polished brass bed surrounded by his sorrowing family and admirers. His fine soft hands pick at the coverlet, which is fashioned of many squares of rich velvet embroidered in feather stitching and edged with a heavy fringe of yellow silk. His handsome grizzled beard fans out on the quilt, and the side whiskers which frame his large florid face are spread carefully over the lace-edged pillow. His favourite niece, the one who is expecting to inherit his considerable fortune, has just finished brushing them with his ebony-backed silver-initialled hairbrushes.

Anne Szumigalski

As the old woman watches her former self, she sees him lift his hand and bless his family and friends with a noble gesture. A bell tinkles, and the servant who has been kneeling modestly beside the great mahogany commode gets quietly to his feet and opens the door.

In sweeps the cardinal, attended by three young acolytes: one to carry the holy oils, one to swing the smoking censor, one to ring the little bell and carry in his other hand the tall lighted candle that will be extinguished when the famous man is declared dead by the family doctor. The cardinal, in his most splendid vestments, bears the Holy Viaticum which the dying man is to receive in preparation for his entry into the next world.

The old woman lies on her hard pallet feasting her inner eye on this glorious scene. How different it is from her present death. This time just two old crones have come to bid her goodbye. She can hear them now in the kitchen enjoying a sad cup of tea and rifling the biscuit box. In the plain little bedroom, the fire has gone out for lack of coal, and the poor woman cannot tell whether the cold she feels creeping up from her feet is the chill of death or simply the November frost penetrating the thin walls of the house.

The village doctor is at the door, to do what I can for the poor creature, she hears him whisper to one of the old biddies on the other side of the partition. When the older of the two gossips ushers him into the bedroom, the dying woman waves him away. I haven't as much as a penny in the house to pay you with, doctor, so be off and take your nasty potions with you. After a few laboured breaths she adds more gently, but please be good enough, if you are passing the rectory, to ask the priest to call.

This long speech so exhausts her that she falls back senseless on the hard grey pillow, and the two crones begin to mutter the prayers for the dead. They are just about to pull the threadbare blanket over her face when the doctor, who has been listening with his ear to her chest, pronounces her still alive.

Perhaps the young priest can be forgiven for dawdling a little on receiving the old woman's message. He has ministered to this village for three years already, and has officiated at three christenings and two weddings, but has never yet been called upon to administer the last rites of the Church. Indeed, he has never known death to visit this place where rosy children grow up into rudely healthy men and women and where old pensioners sit outside their cottages on sunny days knitting and chatting until their century is past.

Excitement is in the air as the priest walks solemnly through the village clothed in a clumsy country-made surplice and carrying the Blessed Sacrament veiled with a scrap of homespun. Men doff their caps. Women fall to their knees on the chilly stones, murmuring almost-forgotten prayers. The young man is enjoying the drama of the occasion and does not hurry. It is only afterwards that he realizes that not one of his parishioners has asked who the dying person might be.

At last he comes to the end of the village and enters the old woman's cottage. He is barely in time, has hardly dipped his finger into the holy oil when the soul leaves the body and flies up into the rafters where it roosts on a crossbeam above the narrow bed. From there it gazes down upon the dead old woman whose white hair sticks out all around her head like a crown of thorns.

Anne Szumigalski

As soon as the priest has left, the two friends wash the withered old body and clothe it in a worn linen shift, which is the only suitable garment they can find in the house. Then they rummage in all the cupboards and the drawers, looking for a few little things to remember her by. The elder hides the tea caddy and a framed holy picture under her ample skirts, while the younger finds two spoons and a tin locket in the shape of a heart. These she tucks away in her reticule and carries home.

Now it is time for the soul, too, to leave the house. It flutters desperately in the eaves and around the door lintel, for in all the excitement no one has remembered to open the window for it to escape and fly back to its creator. It is forced to remain in the house for several days, strutting about on the cold floor and roosting in the rafters.

At last the carpenter and his son come, bringing the rough pine coffin which is to be the old woman's last bed, and the imprisoned soul is able to escape through the open door.

But it does not fly away immediately. It rests for a little while on the topmost twigs of the tall elm which grows behind the cottage. From there it can see the whole village with its neat rows of whitewashed houses, every one with a well-kept backyard from which the winter's supply of carrots and potatoes has recently been dug. At the bottom of each garden is a small bonfire, for the villagers are a tidy lot and do not care to see fallen leaves scuttering about the street and the village pump all winter.

Today there is no wind. From each little fire a thin twist of smoke rises straight upward toward the frosty sky.

Himself and the Virgin

When she wakes, it is no surprise to see him standing there at the foot of the bed, no surprise that he is, or seems to be, human, a man.

For as long as she can remember she has known that he was approaching. She has known this even before she could see so much as a dot on the line of distance.

And he has, after all, been patient enough. Sometimes his pace has speeded a little, sometimes it has slowed. Slow Fox she called this entity as she danced around the living room with her dad—slow, slow, quick quick, slow—it had taken her a long time to learn that. At first she had wanted to do only the fast bits. They had made her feel so excited, so giddy—quickquick quickquick quickquick.

At six she encountered him as a virus, the pain and exhaustion, the nightie soaked in sweat, the cold drink from her mother's cold hand.

Anne Szumigalski

At eight she recognized him as the bacillus peering back at her from the other end of her brother's microscope. At ten, through a telescope, she spied him as a small lone star pricking the distant cloth of night.

Then from baskets and vases, spilled out on shelves and tabletops, spore of fern, seed of poppy. In flowerpots faint wiggle of mite and tick, hop of leaf-miner, darting of fungus gnat. Something always coming nearer, getting larger.

At twelve she saw him as a single bird, one of a vast flock, winging its way over the ocean, falling exhausted on the shore, resting for days on the far edge of the continent.

That's when she decided to sleep a hundred years, more or less, wrapped in the muslin of her dreams, so as not to fret at his slow passage.

Today her lust has awakened her. For five minutes she silently watches him just standing there, staring hotly into her eyes. Then, what did you bring me, she asks. What, not a mushroom, not a flower, not even a map of the Universe?

She doesn't, of course, expect an answer, or a gift for that matter. This is a man of glass, she realizes. It's not difficult to see through him. His satanic intentions.

She smiles. He leaps upon the bed. She strikes him with the only weapon she has—an idea for a dream, a plan for the last journey, that inevitable dance. From now on, she tells him, we will always move hand in hand, both in the same direction.

Never again will they suffer the anxieties, the constraints, the excitement of their long-feared, their long-desired meeting.

The Web—A Conversation

PITCH *and* TOSS

P. What's that?

T. What?

P. On your arm.

T. A bite.

P. Someone bit you?

T. A spider—the Spider.

P. The great Arachnid.

T. The very same. See the tiny fang marks, see the little holes where the venom went in? If only she could have killed me she would, but she was too small. I had to ask myself, in all creation is there a spider big enough to kill and eat a person?

P. Like you.

T. Or you.

P. How about a venomous lion? That would do it.

T. Or simply another venomous person. One with a bite full of spite. One nip and . . .

P. You'd be a goner.

T. Or you.

P. There was once a man who was bitten by a man and . . .

T. And what? Go on.

P. And he died.

T. Which one? Which one died?

P. That's the question. One of them died, but which one. The biter or the bitten.

T. That's a difficult choice. Better they both died.

P. Well, that does seem fairer.

T. But when was life fair?

P. Or death.

T. Exactly. When was anything fair?

P. That's not the point. Things are meant to be equitable. That's the law.

T. What law?

P. The law . . .

T. . . . of averages, you were about to say? That takes a long time to get to equality.

P. But in the end it will.

T. The end of the World.

P. No no. For that you'll have to wait for the end of the Universe.

T. That'll be a long wait.

P. And besides I've heard lately . . .

T. . . . that there's more than one universe.

P. No one has said how many. An infinite number.

T. That thing with the dot, you mean.

P. Yes, the dot. Precisely.

T. How can an infinite number be precise?

P. It could try. It could do its best.

T. It would fail.

P. Like the biter . . .

Anne Szumigalski

T. . . . or the spider . . .

P. . . . or the bitten . . .

T. . . . or the universe . . . .

P. What's that floating in the bathtub?

T. Yuck. It's the spider. She drowned.

P. You drowned her.

T. I didn't do it. It was the water. The water drowned her.

P. Soapy water.

T. A clean death.

P. And there'll be others.

T. Lots of others.

P. Too many, perhaps.

T. They could multiply . . .

P. . . . on and on. They could take over . . .

T. . . . the whole caboodle . . .

P. . . . everything. Every little thing. Even . . .

T. . . . the dot.

Dreamers

She awakens and is glad of it. The dream has been so long, so dull. She has been walking in a London park watching the children play on the grass, watching little boys and old men sail their damn boats on the artificial lake. Who cares, she said to herself over and over, just get me out of this.

She is getting old. She knows it. In fact, it has been going on for some time, and the nightly excitement of her dreams is just about the only amusement left to her, a roller-coaster of adventures in strange lands and violent people, narrow escapes and heroic rescues, tossing on the high seas of an abidingly explicit imagination. She often longs for the night. The dullness of everyday life, the continuous intricate blah blah blah of TV dramas—these can never compare to the excitements and adventures of her sleeping life. And now this. Her dreams have suddenly become as flat and boring as everything else. Bad enough that one's life is a long trail of nothingness—but one's dreams? There should surely be some compensation in one's dreams.

Night after night it is the same thing. She seems to be living the boring life of a middle-class British housewife of undoubted worthiness and dullness. Isn't this what she had hoped to escape by moving to Western Canada, to the wide-open Prairies, in her youth? And yes, she is, or has once been, an adventurous person. What has she done to deserve such an ignominious dream life?

Once or twice she tries staying up all night and sleeping in the daytime. This doesn't improve anything. Indeed, it simply makes things worse. On these occasions, she simply dreams that she is a dull old woman sleeping her way through a chilly damp London night. She is forced (in her dream) to get up and make herself a cup of tea and a hot water bottle. All this is telling on her health, and certainly on her temper. A good thing, she thinks, that she's a widow and lives alone. Heaven only knows what crotchety behaviour an unfortunate partner would have to put up with. And anyway, who on earth would want to live with a woman with such excruciatingly dull dreams?

One night as her dream self comes in from her daily walk in the park to the cluttered but clean, boring London flat where she lives, as she passes the coat hooks and the somewhat speckled hall mirror, she chances to glance at herself and the awful truth becomes clear at once. The face she sees is not hers. It is her sister's round, rather saggy, self-satisfied face which she sees there—Bunface she had always called her—bunfaced Bridget—otherwise, and quite rightly, known as Bunny. So this is it. Some glitch had happened, and she is being forced to live Bunny's totally boring existence. Her dream time has been invaded by a dusty bourgeois reality. Naturally, she is very angry.

And it's surprising how anger can liven the mind, perhaps you might say even the life, of the angry person. The woman can feel her toes tingle and her nose redden with the exertion of her fury. In fact, she begins to

Anne Szumigalski

feel better immediately, and she tells herself it is the realization of the reason for her anger that has livened things up. Now she had someone to be angry with. Someone to blame for her malaise. Bunny, bloody Bunny, she murmurs over and over to herself, bloody Bunny.

And it's so unfair. Bunny is probably taking on her life. Lucky Bunny. Getting up at eight every morning and dragging on her snow boots and buttoning up her jacket, then down to the store through the snow for milk and cigarettes. And the local paper. Feeding the birds, watching the birds, doing the crossword, wondering whether birds have crosswords, or cross-songs of their own, and if they do, can they ever solve them—solve them completely, that is, not just take a stab at them, work the whole thing out to the last tweet?

It's not as though there is nothing to be done about this situation. She'll show Bridget a thing or two. She'll start by going next door where a young couple lives; she'll go there and ring the bell, and when Linda Beeker comes to the door she'll throw a handful of snow in her face and ask her why she is sleeping with the mailman. That should start something. Then she'll get on the bus at the back end without paying the fare and once downtown she'll go into the Bay and do a little shoplifting. If she's blatant and gleeful enough about it, that should get her arrested in no time. What will priggy Bunny make of that, then? The goody-goody one, the one who always tattle-taled to Mummy and Daddy, never mind to the teacher?

And when the police come, she'll lie down on the floor and make them drag her to the paddy wagon. At the station she won't answer any questions, she'll just shriek curses at everybody and spit. She'll insult the. . . . And she begins to wonder what the inside of the Police Station looks like. She's never actually been inside. Do they have cells? Do the cells have those rude toilets in the corner like on TV? Surely not, that's probably just Americans.

While she's speculating, she's pulling on her snow boots again, throwing on an old parka of her husband's. It somehow seems so much more satisfactory than her own pink down jacket. She doesn't do up the zipper; after all, she'll simply have to unzip it again at the cop shop, won't she, and she knows that zipper, it sticks terribly—always did, even years ago when Jack got it new.

No one answers her frantic knocking at #8. Suppose you're having sex in there, she yells, and begins kicking at the door. No one is about. It's too cold and too early in the day. Sex sex sex, she yells. No answer. Just the thud of her boot at the door.

Just then Linda's cat comes round the corner, a handsome Tom whose well-groomed tabby coat and long firm white whiskers she has often admired— looking to catch a few birds are you, she shrieks—you're just like the rest—violence and sex, that's all you think about—and not surprisingly as she throws her snow bomb, which the cat quite artfully dodges, she falls flat on her face in the snow. For a moment she lies there hardly able to breathe, then slowly turns over and makes a snow angel wing with her left arm and then with her right.

She coughs and spits, and tears of melted snow run down her face. Fuck you Bridget, she says very quietly so that only the cat and her sister can hear—put that in your dream—and she lies back in the snow and laughs, or is she crying, she really can't tell which.

Anne Szumigalski

Viaticum—The Text

On the first morning we saw a road stretching before us, and this road was one long word reaching from here to there. How enticingly clear and simple this seemed. At once we packed bread and cheese and knives and skins of fresh water and set out with a will upon our journey.

At the close of that day the road and the word came to an end, and we struck camp for the night. On the second day there was another road and another word. And so it went on. At the end of the sixth day, however, things were a little different. Because we had stopped on our way to pick the service berries that grew by the side of the road, we arrived late at our camping place. It was already dusk, and we were so tired that we threw ourselves down on the grassy verge without so much as taking off our boots or washing our faces. Indeed, we were so tired that we even forgot our evening prayer to the Demiurge Y, he who had undoubtedly arranged this journey for us and watched over us as we travelled.

When we awoke, the midmorning sun was hot upon our upturned faces. Above us, in the blue dome of the sky, there was not a single cloud, simply a sentence made up of all the words from the past week. The message was simple and direct. As soon as we read it, we fell into momentary despair, for up to then we had thought ourselves innocent, or almost so. Surely we were not deserving of such a judgement.

There was no road and no direction. Would there ever be again? Here we were in the wilderness with no one to guide us. Though our hearts beseeched the Demiurge, he did not heed us. Well, there was nothing for it but to make the best of things, and so we lazed through the day in the long fragrant grass. Even the insects joined us in our rest, and nipped at our skin so gently that we hardly noticed their bites.

Of course, Y did not allow us more than one day of rest. The next morning we were off again, pursuing the word and the truth with a little less enthusiasm than before, yet still curious to know where the road would eventually lead us.

Now the pattern was set, and we continued for what seemed like centuries in the same way. On every seventh day the week's words were added to those already crowding the sky, and every sentence was more difficult and threatening than the last one. It was not surprising that the Demiurge had decreed a sabbath of rest. We could imagine that it could take him a whole day to compose a suitably abusive judgement for the next week's journey.

As for us mortals, we were glad to stop on the road to fill our flasks with fresh spring water and to enjoy the

Anne Szumigalski

scenery and the warm sunny weather. When cool evening fell, we began our sabbath dance, watching the shadows of our gestures move gracefully under the moon.

Y was obviously not at all pleased with our light-heartedness, for his words became every week more forbidding and his path more rigorous. In some places it was overgrown with thorny weeds, and in others it was ankle deep in stinking brackish water. Our creator had made up his mind that we were to travel among the sharp stones, grasping at stinging nettles and even at poison ivy if we were so foolish as not to recognize its trinity.

One Wednesday morning as we were wandering along a flinty road that passed through a rock-strewn valley, the enamel sky, which must have become over-burdened with the many curses and judgements written upon it, cracked and split into a thousand thousand pieces. One moment the sky was full of words, the next flakes of blue were falling upon the earth like scurf from the unwashed heads of angels.

And these flakes floated down upon the grass and the stones and the hills and the rivers and the bitter oceans. They alighted, too, on the birds and the beasts, even upon our friends the insects. And from this falling all creation received its voice. Never was there such a roaring and a twittering and a buzzing and a squealing. As for us poor wanderers, we too received this blessing. Our ears and our mouths were opened and we shouted and sang and argued until our throats were sore.

Now there could be no more sky words and no more need for us to travel the earth. This was the place of our deliverance. We made up our minds to settle in this spot and to build a city with the stones that lay around us. Here we live still, passing the days in discussions and quarrels and the evenings in the singing of bawdy ballads and the telling of tall tales.

No longer are we confined to gesture and the written word. Indeed we have almost forgotten how to read and write, so happy are we with the speeches and lies which come effortlessly to our tongues.

As for our master the Demiurge, he has been defeated by his own cruelty and arrogance, for he among all beings did not receive a voice. The sky of words fell downward only, and Y was far too proud to descend from his heaven and accept the gift of speech. In his high place he is silent still, though every now and then he throws down his orders or curses in a written scroll or codex. Of course, we never read these, for we are far too busy chatting and boasting and reciting for that.

However, we are not entirely lacking in piety. In the very centre of our city we have built a modest temple to contain these holy objects. Sometimes one of our children, with the natural curiosity of the young, demands to learn to read and to discover the secrets locked up in those pages. Then we explain that our revered creator, Yaldabaoth the Demiurge, has promised to punish with terrible severity the impious fool who dares disturb the dusty silence that lies forever on his words.

Anne Szumigalski

Mates

Two young women are walking arm in arm up the high street; they work in a shoe factory and have just got their first pay cheques. Now they are off to the shops to buy skirts and cardigans of loganberry wool knit, also some gauzy underwear and stockings and other falderals. They are chatting and laughing as they go, for they are very good friends and never tire of one another's company.

A man rides by on his bike. As he passes the two friends he can't resist turning his head for another look, for they are such a charming pair with their shining hair and teeth and their sturdy legs in flesh-coloured stockings.

It would be a shame, the young man thinks, to court and marry one of them and take her away from her mate, then both of them would be unhappy. For who would find time to chat so amiably about the diets they were on or about the courses they were planning to take at the Technical Institute?

What I should do, he decides, is to fly away with both of them to the South Seas. There we could all live together in a grass hut by the seashore. The girls can chat all day as they pick breadfruit and deck each other's hair with hibiscus blossoms.

And he's happy, too. Every day he fishes in the lagoon. Every night he lies between the two friends on a soft mattress of palm fronds. Whichever way he turns, there is always a lovely young thing ready to greet him with open arms.

All the same, a man can get to feel trapped by a life like this. Could he, for instance, ever get away without their noticing? Well, he must just wriggle ever so carefully to the bottom of the bed and escape without waking either of them.

And so one night he creeps quietly out of the grass hut and hails a passing ship, which takes him back to the murky North. There he finds a job in a factory making small engine parts.

Each morning he gets up very early and makes himself a piece of toast and a cup of tea. Then he wheels his bicycle out of the shed and rides off to work through the dark deserted streets.

Anne Szumigalski

Morning

In the attic of a small house a man and a woman are lying side by side in an old brass bed. They are not quite touching. A beam of morning sunlight strikes through the dormer window, lighting the dip of blue cotton quilt between them. The beam has the shape of a curved knife.

The woman turns her face toward the wall, but the man remains staring at the motes dancing in the shaft of light. This is a universe, or perhaps only a narrow galaxy. The motes are stars twirling in their own light, each star encircled by planets.

The surface of every planet is covered with seas and forests, with farmlands and cities. In each city are rows upon rows of small houses whose walls are painted white inside and out, whose stairs are twisting and carpeted.

In each attic is a bed where a man and a woman are lying side by side under a pieced coverlet. A curved beam of sunlight separates them. Either they will turn toward each other into a warm embrace or they will move apart, and, as the sun climbs higher, a valley of blue patchwork will grow cold between them.

The Tower

A man built a tower in a field. Just why should he do that?

Well, the Prairie is full of follies: this half-a-wall petering out after a hundred yards or so, that house built of Coca-Cola cans, that elegant wooden ship with nowhere to sail but across the waves of grassland. There are small towns which are nothing but names on brave boards freshly painted each spring—by whom, for whom? Then there are ditches meant once as the beginning of great canals, but abandoned after a few days digging, and small stunted woodlands once projected as great forests through which imagined herds of huge wood buffalo would one day roam at will. A medium-sized round tower built of fieldstones: is that so foolish then?

Like most things on the flatlands, you can see this tower from a long way off. If the fellow who built it wanted to hide himself, why would he construct anything so obvious? If he wanted simply to show off, why did he build it so far from any hamlet or farmstead?

He had his reasons, of course, and they were sad ones. This unfortunate young man, though he was not

Anne Szumigalski

bad-looking at all and made a more than adequate income, had been jilted twice, and after this doubly ignominious experience had made up his mind never to have any more concourse with women. He decided to build himself a home out on the Lone Prairie and conduct the rest of his life from that point both of solitude and advantage.

And yes, this situation did have a certain advantage—a double advantage, in fact. First, he was an architect by trade, and could therefore design a tower that was both commodious and beautiful. Second, as long as he had all the tools of his trade about him, he could conduct his business from his residence, the tower.

All he needed to make his life tolerable was one ally, and that ally, of course, had to be the mailman. One who would be in duty bound to visit him at least once a week, delivering and collecting his mail—not that he received or sent out any letters except business letters and the designs and plans for his work.

Luckily, the mailman was quite amenable, for a small consideration, to bring him his week's groceries with the mail. All these were pulled up in the dumb waiter he had constructed on the outside of the tower for just this purpose. In fact, it was nothing more than a hefty wooden box drawn up and down by pulleys and ropes operated by hand, and that only from above.

When he had pulled up the mail and his provisions, the architect would send down his outgoing mail and a cheque for the amount he owed his benefactor the postman. That fellow, the father of several growing children, was very happy with this arrangement, which afforded him a little extra income without too much extra work, something the father of a family must always find useful.

This arrangement, then, went on for more than three years, and the architect, who in his lonely tower was quite free from the distractions of the world, became more and more respected in his profession. Indeed, he was very often asked to address conferences or speak to university classes. These invitations he was, of course, always obliged to refuse, on the grounds that he was pressed for time as his work kept him so extremely busy. In fact, this could have gone on for half a century but for the intervention of the Fates.

One Friday, mail day, the architect was waiting as usual by the tower window for the arrival of the mailman. He had everything ready as usual: the outgoing plans in their stiff envelopes, the cheque written out—all but the amount, which the mailman would yell up at him as he placed the box of groceries in the lift with the week's mail—those plans and orders and boxes of drafting supplies which represented the young man's only concourse with the world away from the confines of his tower and the empty prairie landscape.

It was usually about three in the afternoon when the mailman arrived for his weekly visit, and on this particular Friday the architect was at the high window of his tower waiting for the familiar sound of gravel pinging on the metal of the mail truck, for the familiar sight of the cloud of prairie dust advancing, the cloud of dust that would reveal the familiar van approaching along the rough road. The uniformed figure got out and lugged the box of groceries. All was as usual. The architect got ready to pull the ropes to bring the lift to the top of the tower. How heavy it seemed. His arms ached with the exertion. Well, he wasn't getting any younger, he told himself, and perhaps he wasn't getting enough exercise. As he pulled on the ropes, he made a mental note to double the number of push-ups and knee-bends in his daily routine. A man who lives in a tower can expect to get weak, he told himself severely, if he doesn't make a special effort to keep himself in shape.

In fact, he was sweating when at last the box arrived opposite the open window, but when he leaned out and opened the little door to the contraption he was startled to see that it contained not only the usual carton of supplies but the crouched figure of a mail person—a female mail person. This person removed her uniform cap, letting free her profuse mane of golden brown hair. She bowed as gracefully as she could in her bent posture. What was the poor fellow to do? He could hardly leave her there in that uncomfortable position. Before he realized what he was doing, he had taken her hand and pulled her in through the window.

There she stood in the fieldstone tower where no woman had ever stood before. What would she say, he asked himself. How could she possibly explain her unexpected appearance? In fact, she said never a word, simply helped him drag in the box of groceries and handed him his mail which he was too surprised to even glance at. Then she marched boldly into the little galley at the back of the tower and began to put away the groceries. She seemed to know exactly where everything should be stacked, and when she had finished that task she began at once to bang about amongst his bachelor kitchen arrangements with the obvious intention of cooking the supper. Still neither of them spoke. Not a word passed between them. There they sat opposite each other at the small table, eating, nodding, smiling, but neither of them uttering a word. Dusk had fallen, and the architect got up to light the lamp. Who would speak first? Neither of them uttered a single word. Not one word. The next morning it was the architect's turn to cook. The breakfast, to judge by her appetite, was very much to the young woman's taste. What to do now?

The whole weekend was passed in this way. They took turns cooking and tidying and putting things to rights and then sat down opposite each other, he on the kitchen stool, she on the only chair that the place afforded.

There they sat staring into each other's eyes until darkness intervened, and it was again time to go to bed.

The next day was Sunday and the man realized with alarm that his beautiful and silent companion would have to leave him and go back to her life on the outside. He contemplated his options. The question was, did he love this woman more than he loved his tower, this beloved edifice which had afforded him almost three years of blessed solitude? She was sitting there staring into his eyes, obviously asking the same question. If he let her go, would she ever return? His natural caution got the upper hand, and he somehow persuaded himself that, in spite of their obvious feelings for each other, he should avoid making a snap decision. Gravely he handed her his grocery list for the coming week. Solemnly she crawled into the dumb waiter and bent

Anne Szumigalski

double as he let her down foot by foot, the rope burning his hands he held it so tightly.

Then he remembered that, during the whole of this long and interesting weekend, he had quite forgotten his mail which lay in a heap in the far corner of the room.

There would, of course, be the usual plans and suggestions and contracts for his work, but, though he made a great effort, he somehow could not get up much of an interest in them. For a few seconds he just stood there staring at the plastered wall of his tower, almost covered as it was with plans and photographs of the buildings he had designed.

But at the moment it was more important to hurry to the tower window, to lean out as far as he could and to watch the distant turn in the road where the mail truck disappeared at last into a puff of dust.

Fear of Knives

The young woman stands by the window holding something up to the light. It could be a feather from the wing of a dove. It could be the leaf of that lily plant whose blossom, heavy with scent, bends almost to the earth, something she could certainly see through the clear pane if she stood on a chair and looked out.

If the light should fall on this thing, she believes, it will either melt into itself or into the idea of itself, a dagger, that is, a kris, a bright blade.

Soon twilight will fill every part of the room. It will creep out from the corners hiding the pattern on the wallpaper, which is parrots in a tropical forest, hiding the dusty squares where pictures once hung in their frames, in their glory.

She imagines the paintings as battle scenes with horses and chariots and flashing swords, or perhaps the smaller ones were simply illustrations torn from the

Anne Szumigalski

Book of Weapons, badly framed and hung slightly askew. Why, she asks herself, did no one bother to straighten them?

Once, in another house, when they were children, her brother was given a skinning knife for Christmas. She remembers how envy filled up her mind like sour cranberry juice in a cup. She had plotted to somehow wrest that knife from him, but all day he kept it buttoned in the pocket of his jerkin, safe in its sheath.

At night it lay under his pillow with his other treasures, a white stone with a hole in it big enough for a little finger to poke through, a worn Clovis point he had found one day on the pathway to school. These things were of no interest to his sister whose one desire was the blade with the elk-horn handle.

Dark falls at last, and the woman remembers both her desire and her fear. How, if she managed to thrust her hand under the pillow and steal away the knife, she had planned to bury it in a hole in the garden. How she had planned to tell herself as she covered the sharp curve of the blade with damp earth that she was hiding her brother in a place where no one would ever find him again.

The Fall

My father was born in a distant country where every person is a tree—every adult, that is.

Children are field flowers. They are grass. They are lilies and poppies and small blue lupines. Until puberty they are any plants they choose. More than that, they may change their minds as many times as they wish. A child may wake as a gillyflower and go to sleep as eglantine. Is there any wonder that in that country no one is in a hurry to grow up?

At the age of twelve or so, each must name a tree and is stuck with this choice until the tree falls from age, or is struck down by the axe of the woodcutter. This last is their way of explaining the death of the young in battle, for, in spite of their worship of the peaceable plant, they are a warlike lot.

All this my father told me, but though I bothered and cajoled him, he would never say which tree he had chosen or whether, in this new country, he still felt bound by the customs of his birthplace.

He always seemed just a man to me, and very like other people's fathers—that is, strong and infallible in my childhood and, as I advanced into adolescence, more and more clumsy and overbearing. There was one difference, though. Unlike other men, he was never seen without a shirt or a sweater. Not that he was particularly modest in other ways. Several times I caught him pulling on his trousers in a hurry. I had a good look. Nothing strange there.

But what was he hiding beneath his tee-shirts and button-up cardigans? Was he afraid of woodpeckers? Was there a hole there beneath his heart where a squirrel had made her nest?

I was almost a grown woman when he took me for a holiday in a warmer part of the country. It was May and already early summer in that gentle climate. He pointed out a tree I had never seen on the Prairies and acknowledged it as his own. *Hippocastanum*, he explained proudly. Its leaves were huge green hands, and between them sprung tall racemes of bloom like white and yellow candles. This, then, was my father's tree, generous in its spread, amazing in its summer complacency.

We stood there hand in hand as he told me about its various phases, of how in Fall it would bear inedible brown nuts in leathery green cases, nuts that are the weapons of little boys in their battles.

All this was years ago, and my father is dead now, hollowed and fallen like every tree before him. I was with him when he died.

No sooner had he taken his last breath than I leaned over him and began to unbutton his pyjama jacket. What did I expect to find? Simply the chest of an old tired man, the tangles of coarse grey hair intricate as twigs. The nipples hard and resinous as winter buds.

The Winter Cat

I don't agree, says the cat, shifting its position a little on the old woman's foot, I don't agree at all.

That, says the woman, plying her needle between the three layers of cloth in the square she is patching, is because you're a cat. It's different for a woman. Quite different.

Different how? and the cat looks up rather belligerently into the woman's eyes. For once she has looked at the cat, has lifted her eyes from her work. The pattern, if you looked at it one way, was called Tumbling Blocks, if another way, Eastern Star, the colours grey and ivory and a surprising shade of burnt orange—and any prints she's been able to find that complement these colours, in fact, almost the colours of the cat's abundant coat. She certainly has an eye for the garish, the cat muses, turning its face away in the direction of the window. Different how?

The woman has come to a difficult turn in the pattern and doesn't answer right away. In fact, the March evening is drawing in and it's time to light the lamp. Either that or she can put her work aside for a few minutes and try to answer the cat's rather impertinent question.

It's like this, she wants to say. It's like that. But how could a cat understand? It has something to do with, well, love.

The cat makes no attempt to hide its scorn for such a ridiculous answer. If a cat could manage a sceptical smile, it would. As it is it manages to convey a very proper sneer.

The woman foolishly tries to mend matters by going into more and more details—the arm round the shoulders, the hand lightly stroking the breast. The words, I love you, I love you, the faces getting closer, the lips touching, the kiss, the. . . .

But the cat has heard enough already and gets up and stalks arrogantly across the room, leaps upon a chair by the window, pricks up its ears and watches for a few minutes with great attention the shadowy world of the garden and the pathway beyond. The world of night hunting, and of dark rumours, and of course the world of feline sexual encounters. The cat, who is entering its heat, is beginning to feel uneasy and excited, and oh that terrible longing, that inconsolable desire for another wilder life where stealth and cunning are everything.

Beyond the garden and the dirt pathway there is the Wood, a dense thicket of trees and undergrowth just now quickening into spring. A yellowish haze of new leaves clouds the branches of the oaks and elms, and

Anne Szumigalski

the sallows and willows are putting out their upright silvery catkins. It's there that the cat spends its summers. Relishing its freedom. Giving birth to a litter of kittens in the underbrush. And hunting, always hunting, mouse tail and bird wing littering the forest floor around its den. Can there be any more exciting life than that one? In summer the cat forgets the woman who feeds and shelters its winters, who sits and sews and chats by the yellow light of the lamp, who walks out to the gate to pick up the can of milk that the farmer leaves there every morning. Who shares her life and food with the cat. In summer the cat is the Wild Cat of the Woods and that is that.

You might well think that the opposite is true—that in winter the cat is entirely engrossed in its domestic life in the cosy warmth of the house. But that's not quite so—as it sits there enjoying the lamplight and the firelight and the dinner that the woman puts down in the dish marked, absurdly, CAT, in blue on the china rim. (How, after all, can a cat be expected to read—even a cat who can hold a conversation as well as this one ?)

The woman, who is a good deal sharper than the cat imagines, knows very well that her winter companion dreams always of its summer self. Never far from the animal's mind is that other, the hunter, the stalker, the accurate triumphant pouncer.

But there is always another side to every question. every speculation and desire. What does the cat care about the woman's thoughts, for instance? How they go back to her lively youth of assignations and trysts. How she wonders about her lost children, her faint-hearted suitors, her ardent but faithless lovers whose faces appear in her dreams, whose deceitful words echo in her ears still.

One day in early autumn, when the weather is getting cooler and damper, and prey is getting scarcer and more wary, the cat, who is after all a practical creature, decides the time has come to leave its wild existence and take up residence once more in the cottage by the edge of the woods.

When it brushes against the door as the first snow sprinkles the front step, when it jumps up against the door yowling softly and asking to be let in, how can the cat know that the woman for a moment imagines a tall man, bent now perhaps with age, standing there with a faded bouquet of autumn leaves in his hand, a gift for an old flame at last remembered, or perhaps a young woman with a half-remembered face, a shawl-wrapped child sleeping in her arms.

Of course, of course, it is just the usual winter cat. Come in, come in, says the woman in a welcoming way, already her mind going forward to some of the discussions—one might almost call them arguments, she looks forward to having with her friend, who stalks in as though it owns the place—the house, the hearth, the cat dish, even the woman herself, whom the cat imagines to have been longing all summer for its scratch at the door, for its wet paws marking up the just-washed, just-polished bluestones of the cottage floor.

Anne Szumigalski

The Hand—A Conversation

PENNY *and* ANTE

Pen.   Open it, then.

Ant.   What?

Pen.   You know what.

Ant.   Tell me.

Pen.   You know, your hand.

Ant.   Which hand is that?

Pen.   The closed one. The one you are hiding.

Ant.   Left or right?

Pen.   Right.

Ant.   See, it's empty. Nothing there.

Pen.   The other one, then.

Ant.   That's empty, too.

Pen.   You cheated. I saw you. You dropped it into your pocket.

Ant.   Which pocket is that?

Pen.   The one you dropped whatever-it-is into.

Ant. This pocket?

Pen. OK, that one will do. Turn it out. Inside out.

Ant. See. Nothing but a handkerchief and some bus tickets. Here, take a couple. Catch a bus and leave me alone.

Pen. I could catch a cold.

Ant. What do you mean?

Pen. Your filthy rag of a handkerchief. I could catch a cold.

Ant. But you can't catch me. You can't catch me out.

Pen. It's a trick. You're a trickster.

Ant. So.

Pen. What do you mean—so?

Ant. So what. Everything is a trick. That's the nature of existence. Trickery, bribery, chicanery. . . .

Pen. Cheating.

Ant. Just so. Watch now. How do you like this . . .

Pen. . . . trick. You open your hands and they're full of money. You close them and now they're full of dirt. That's the worst trick anyone could play.

Ant. Not quite. I have another one up the sleeve of my shirt. Watch this.

Pen. Things are growing. Something's growing in the dirt.

Ant. That's what dirt's for. That's what trickery's for.

Pen. Your hands are sprouting. Your hands are flowering. O my God.

Ant. That's what I keep telling you. God's a trickster, it's inevitable.

Pen. Is nothing innocent? Not even the flowers? Not even the hands?

Ant. Not even my hands, not even yours.

Anne Szumigalski

Wings

A woman wakens her husband at three a.m. She kicks him gently, and then not so gently. He turns over. She pulls back the bed covers, when he starts to get cold she knows he will stir and try to pull the blankets back over himself. Then she'll have him. She wants him to sit up. She wants him to listen. She wants to tell him about her dream, how the mouse in the cupboard grew wings and flew around the bedroom like a moth. It probably was a moth, says the man grumpily, go back to sleep, Millicent.

The wife, who in fact is called Fanny, wonders if this lapse with her name is something to do with a dream her husband is having or simply his way of getting even for having been awakened at such an hour. Could be both.

Fanny wants to get back to her moth dream, or was it a mouse dream? She ignores this prime opportunity to quarrel and sinks herself deep into sleep. The mouse-moth becomes a very small angel alighting on the left hand bed post and blessing her and her husband Harold with outstretched arms. Even those small arms seem all embracing with their blessing. She smiles rather impatiently in her sleep.

Harold is by now wide awake, and not at all likely to fall asleep for some time. He will have to think of something to while away the next hour or two. If he turns on the light to read, his wife will certainly waken again and tell him more of her banal adventures in dreamland. Naturally, he doesn't want that. Nothing else for it, he is forced to amuse himself with the resources of his own imagination.

He thinks of himself walking on a stony shore. It's a bright day, but the wind is blowing coldly on his face. His beard is becoming crisp with it. He puts up his hand to protect himself, for the wind is not just cold; it has a sharp, salty bite. If he licks his lips he will surely taste the sea.

And it's not surprising that his feet are hurting, for when he looks down he is walking on the stones with bare toes. He remembers his sturdy boots neatly placed side by side under the bed at home. Why didn't he think to put them on before he started out on this expedition? His wife has always laughed at his feet. How white and delicate they are. They spend all their time in socks and shoes, she says, while hers, small and tough and brown, run naked everywhere, up and down stairs, in and out of the garden, even sometimes down the street to the corner store. I may not envy her dreams, he tells himself, but I certainly envy her feet.

A bird is screaming, a shrill two-note call, an urgent call. He looks up and sees the poor thing flagging on the stones with an apparently broken wing. Poor thing. He advances toward the bird, which moves painfully away as he approaches. Just a little at a time, just enough to persuade him to follow it. Just enough, he realizes, to lure him away from its nest. A nest with eggs, no doubt, and it must be somewhere by his feet. Those pale feet with their pathetic curved toes. Painful toes. Much as he wants to find that nest, to steal one of those plover's eggs, something he as never seen, has certainly never held in his hand, the pain is too great. He will simply have to come out of his reverie and go back for his boots. Heaven knows whether he'll ever find again that shore, that ocean, that certain bird with that certain nest, that particular perfect pale egg scribbled and blotched with black.

By now Fanny is wide awake and has padded on her small brown feet down to the kitchen and is filling the kettle for tea, for who can sleep with all this going on? She had wanted to dream of wings, she explains as she hands him his cup with the bluebirds flying round the rim (hers has swallows). She had tried very hard for butterflies, but that hadn't worked, then dragonflies, and then a flock of waxwings lighting on a rowan tree. Nothing had been really satisfactory. Angels? Yes, but angels are getting so common these days. You can hardly go down as far as the meat market without encountering one, or perhaps even two walking arm in arm up the high street. No, when she has finished her tea, she will cuddle down and have another go at butterflies.

But Harold, sipping carefully at his tea which is just too hot to drink comfortably, is off again on his wondering ways. Do angels lay eggs? If they do, what colour are they? Perhaps they are shining, translucent, speckled with gold. Perhaps the folded wings of the cherub are visible when you hold the egg up to the light. And perhaps the mother angel sings eternally on the shore to distract you from her nest, her pinions lamely hanging down in a vain pretence of brokenness.

Fear of Knives

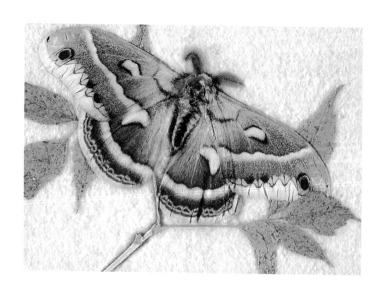

A Woman Gets Up

at the very moment of dawn. At her end of the world it has just become summer, a time when light comes early and always a sharp breeze with it. Nevertheless, she opens her window, and her ear picks up what may be a whistle or a cry. There sits recollection in the shape of a small drab bird clinging to the bough of her rowan, feathers of dust, voice of dry seeds.

How can the little creature have found this place: how can it have known exactly which tree to alight on? These are her questions.

Perhaps if she'd risen even earlier she could have observed the coming of the bird and been able to study its method of navigation. Certainly, she would have seen its struggles against the foreign air, its fall into the grass, where for several minutes it flapped vainly against the damp blades, then gamely leapt up to the slick grey bough, where it rested its tired head amongst the uncomfortable leaf buds.

As she muses on this, the bird turns its small shrewd eyes toward the window and recognizes her. Now quite sure of its destination, it begins to explain the woman to herself in a gentle muddled twittering.

The Hat— A Conversation

PICK *and* CHOOSE

P. So you're leaving?

Ch. What gives you that idea?

P. You're wearing a hat. A woolly hat. You must be going out. No one wears a woolly hat in the house.

Ch. My ears were cold. I wanted. . . .

P. What you wanted was to sneak out without saying a word.

Ch. A word like goodbye? You expected me to say goodbye?

P. Why not? People do. People do say goodbye. So long. See you.

Ch. Alright, then. Goodbye.

P. That's it? Nothing else? Like thanks? Like thanks for everything?

Ch. What everything? Lunch—

P. and dinner, and breakfast and cups of tea and five years of—

Ch. misery. You know it was misery.

P. We talked a lot. We always talked a lot.

Ch. Blah blah blah.

Anne Szumigalski

P. Conversation is important. Thirty percent of couples split up because they never—

Ch. discuss things? I read that book, too. The difference, is I don't believe everything I read. Scribble scribble scribble. This guru and that friendly psychologist. What do they know?

P. They've studied people. People's relationships, that kind of thing. They must have learned something.

Ch. They've never studied us. They've never had to live with you and your endless conversation, year in and year out. Blah blah. I can think of better things to do than listen to you blabbing out your anxieties and premonitions.

P. I don't have them.

Ch. Premonitions?

P. Anxieties.

Ch. In other words, you don't care. You don't give a damn. You never have.

P. You're crying. Those are tears on your cheeks. Here, take my hankie.

Ch. Your filthy hankie.

P. It's not filthy. It's a clean one from this morning. See, it's still folded. You can still see where the initial is folded over.

Ch. I don't believe it. My initial. My hankie. You stole my hankie.

P. I just borrowed it. It was the only clean one I could find.

Ch. My hankie. The one my aunt sent me for Christmas.

P. You weren't using it. I thought you wouldn't mind. I thought we were. . . .

Ch. Next you'll be borrowing my toothbrush.

P. I thought we were. . . .

Ch. We were. But we're not any more. I'm going upstairs to pack.

P. You were leaving without packing?

Ch. I wasn't leaving. I was just trying on this hat. Do you think the colour suits me?

P. Orange? I don't think orange is really your thing.

Ch. There's a green one in the hall closet.

P. That's more your colour. You do have a green tinge in your eyes.

Ch. Hazel.

P. Is that her name?

Ch. Who?

P. Your girlfriend. The one you were running away with.

Ch. If I had a girlfriend, her name would certainly not be Hazel.

P. So what would it be, then? Penelope, Marian, Dolores, Jane, Mercy. . . ?

Ch. . . . pity, peace.

P. Pax, as they say. Now, whose turn is it to make lunch?

Anne Szumigalski

The Cloud

A woman is cleaning old hens for the pot. She stands at the kitchen sink looking over a mown paddock, where her son is dawdling his way home from school.

In the low sun blessing his head, she sees a halo of flames consuming his wild shag of hair.

Fright rises in her gullet like a mouthful of mushrooms, perhaps poisonous, perhaps merely inedible.

The boy sits in the grass, knees to chin, picking at the tiny dark dots on his legs. Each one conceals a hidden coil of hair, ready to erupt as the flake of skin is lifted.

He's thinking of hay time, the swing of his uncle's scythe, the picnic under the hedge, and his mother's voice telling once again the story of when he was three and almost fell down the well.

He's heard it all before, how this field was then a simple pasture where ancient Edda grazed out her final years. Her only duty was to carry him once a day round the paddock, past the tall copper beech to the door of the house and his mother's arms. That last time the old donkey lost her footing on the slippery scatter of empty masts, tossed him to the very brink of the open well.

If, his mother keeps saying, you had been one pound heavier. If Agnes had not been standing there, winching up a bucketful. But he cannot remember the incident.

Of the animal he recalls only weathered droppings, fading year by year into the litter behind the broken lean-to, until they disappeared.

Tonight, he decides, he will ask to camp out in the paddock. The old shed can be his tent.

Anne Szumigalski

That mildewed place, his mother will say, and she'll hand him a sooty kettle. Better make a fire, brew up. You could catch something.

The very words she'd said that other time in town, when he'd stopped to speak with a grey labouring man warming his hands over a brazier, where two ashy potatoes roasted side by side in the failing embers. As sure as eggs is eggs, she'd said, pulling him away, you could catch something. It's easy done.

Now she's emptying the last bird, pulling the trail from the scratchy hollow of the carcass, watching the child get up from the grass and run toward the house. Mother, Mother, he's shouting.

She doesn't answer, sees only the blistered arms, the trouser legs neatly pinned over the stumps of thighs, her own trembling hand carrying a spoonful of porridge to the helpless mouth.

She drops the spoon into the empty bowl, then rummages in the dresser drawer for a strong white comb, begins the slow untangling of his hair.

Must be getting on, she said to herself in the morning, must be old age coming on. All through her married life, all through her long widowhood, she had slept through the night without so much as a bad dream to disturb her, and now this.

She had, in fact, awakened in darkness, just as the moon was rising. Something had induced her to the window to look out. There, standing by the gate, was a man, a young man by the look of him, staring up at her window. She could not, of course, make out his face, as the rowan tree by the gate cast too many shadows, but yes, he seemed by his stature, by his stance, to be a young man, a tall and well-set-up young man, the very kind who would have the effrontery to be standing out there in the middle of the night staring up at her house.

Now, she was a person of very modest means, you could almost call her poor, and so she was not at all afraid that the fellow was a thief come in the night to rob her. What, indeed, would he get for his pains? A loaf of bread, a hunk of cheese? Her mother's old tea pot with the broken spout? He hardly looked starving. Just yearning, and perhaps curious. What could he be looking for, what?

Well, she was not about to spend the night wondering. She sensibly hopped back into her warm bed and fell immediately into a satisfying, dreamless sleep.

That would have been that; she would have forgotten the incident, had it not reoccurred every night while there was enough moonlight to awaken her. Every night the same young man. Every night she awakened to the same desire to look out her window. It was getting to be a habit. And a bad habit, at that. Next time, she told herself. Tonight, if it happens again, I will simply stay in bed; I won't get up. Why should I get up to stare at a strange man in my front yard? That's probably what he wants. For me to get up and stare through the window. He wants to frighten me. Well, I just won't be frightened.

But that night she awakened with the same curiosity. Would the young fellow be there by the gate? What did he want? This time, she would fool him. She wouldn't look out the window; she would simply throw a shawl over her shoulders and go out and find out what he was about. She would go out there and confront him. Young man, she would say, who are you and what do you want?

Hadn't she read somewhere that nothing unnerves a young man more than a far-from-timid old lady with a loud voice? She practised her speech several times— Young man who are you? What do you want?—Perhaps that was not fierce enough, perhaps, What the hell do you want? Too fierce. Young man, what are you doing here? You are stepping in my flowerbed. This is my property. Go away at once.

When she got downstairs, unlocked her door, and went out, she was surprised how chilly it was out there. It was years, she realized, since she had gone out after sunset. Many years. The garden, the gate, the road beyond: all looked quite different in the moonlight. When she got to the gate she looked back at the house. A cosy cottage, well-tended—that's what you would have said about it in the daytime.

No young man this time. Perhaps she had simply imagined him, had made him up out of the shadows the tree cast over the gate and pathway.

When she looked up at the house it was different, she decided. The same door, the same window, but who was that at the window? It was, indeed, the young man. Now he was looking out and she looking in. Not a situation that pleased her. Perhaps now she would at least get a good look at his face, that face that she had come to think of as her one desire in life. There he stood. Even leaning out the window toward her, she still couldn't make out his features. What a fool I was. She told herself to turn out the light. Now I will never know who the rascal is. And she began to laugh, and the young man at the window laughed too. His rather thin shrill laugh. A funny laugh for such a fine young man, she said to herself.

A Conversation

TO calls FRO up from the void

Fro Adsum.

To You just think you're here.

Fro What do you mean, I just think I'm here?

To Well, you are simply a figment of my—

Fro imagination, you were going to say?

To I was going to say intellect. A figment of my mind.

Fro You like that word, don't you—figment. You think you're clever using words like that. Makes you sound smart, knowing.

To Well what do *you* know? You who are simply—

Fro something you have dreamed up? Somebody you've invented just to have an adversary. Someone to quarrel with.

To Not quarrel. I just want to argue. I like that. I love a good argument. Now, what shall be the subject of our argument? It took a lot of effort to think of you, and now I want you to think.

Fro So now I'm your servant. You want me to think. You want me to argue.

To Let's call it a discussion. A discussion is more civilized than an argument.

Anne Szumigalski

Fro   You imagine you are civilized? You imagine I'll go along with that. Get lost.

To   I can't. I'm a real person. I can lose you, but I can't lose myself.

Fro   You could die.

To   I'm not ill. What am I supposed to die of?

Fro   You could have an accident.

To   I don't drive.

Fro   You could fall downstairs.

To   This house doesn't have stairs.

Fro   You could start a fire.

To   I don't smoke.

Fro   That's a lie. What about last Sunday after church? A cigar no less, a very expensive cigar.

To   A present from my uncle.

Fro   Which uncle?

To   Uncle Harold.

Fro   Go on, you haven't got an Uncle Harold. You're making the whole thing up. There's Uncle Basil and Uncle James and Uncle Bertie, but I never heard of Uncle Harold.

To   My aunt, then.

Fro   Aunts don't give cigars. You know better than that.

To   She just had a baby.

Fro   You're lying again. Can you never stick to the facts? How can we have a good argument— discussion—if you never stick to the facts?

To   You're not even a fact. You're a fiction.

Fro   First I'm a figment and then I'm a fiction. Make up your mind.

To   Which mind?

Fro   Exactly.